WITHDRAWN

For
Jo, Ollie, Rufus, Ben,
Rob and Rosie

First published 2010 by Walker Books Ltd
87 Vauxhall Walk, London SE11 5HJ

2 4 6 8 10 9 7 5 3 1

© 2010 Lucy Cousins

The right of Lucy Cousins to be identified as author/illustrator of this work has been asserted by her in accordance with the Copyright, Designs and Patents Act 1988

This book has been typeset in Futura.
Handlettering by Lucy Cousins.

Printed in China.

British Library Cataloguing in Publication Data:
a catalogue record for this book is available from the British Library

ISBN 978-1-4063-2368-9

www.walker.co.uk

I'm the Best

Lucy Cousins

WALKER BOOKS
AND SUBSIDIARIES

LONDON • BOSTON • SYDNEY • AUCKLAND

Hello,
I'm Dog and I'm
the best.

These are my friends —
Ladybird, Mole, Goose and
Donkey.

I love them.
They're brilliant,
but I'm the best.

I can run much faster than Mole.

I can dig holes much better than Goose. I WON.

I'm the best.

I'm much bigger than Ladybird.

I won.
I'm the best.

I can swim much better than Donkey.

I won. I'm the best.

I'm the best at everything.

I feel a bit sad.

I can dig holes much longer and much deeper than you, Dog.

So I won.

I'm the best.

Actually, I can swim much faster than you, Dog.
So I won. I'm the best.

Actually,
I'm much bigger
than you, Dog.

So I won.
I'm the best.

Actually,
I can fly much
    better than you, Dog.

In fact you don't
even have wings.
So I won.
    I'm the best.

Oh dear.
I'm not best at
anything.

I'm rubbish at everything.

I'm just a silly SHOW OFF.

I don't even have wings.

And I'm mean to my friends.

Sorry, Ladybird.
Sorry, Mole.
Sorry, Goose,
Sorry, Donkey.

Don't worry.

You are the best at being our
best friend.

And you are the best at
having beautiful
fluffy ears.

And we love you.

Oh phew!

Obviously having beautiful fluffy ears is the most important thing.

So I AM the best.